The Con

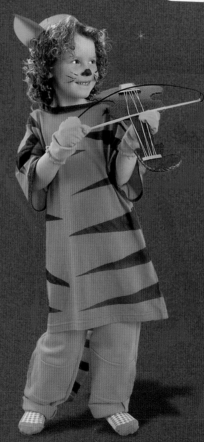

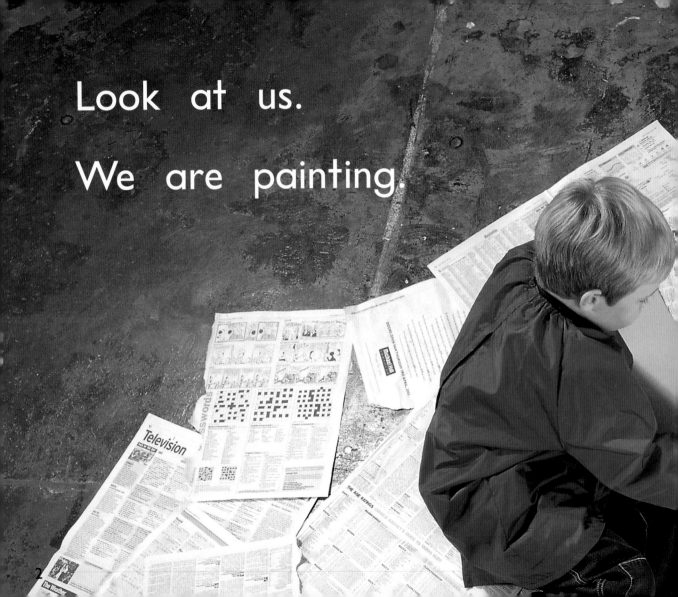

Look at us.

We are painting.

2

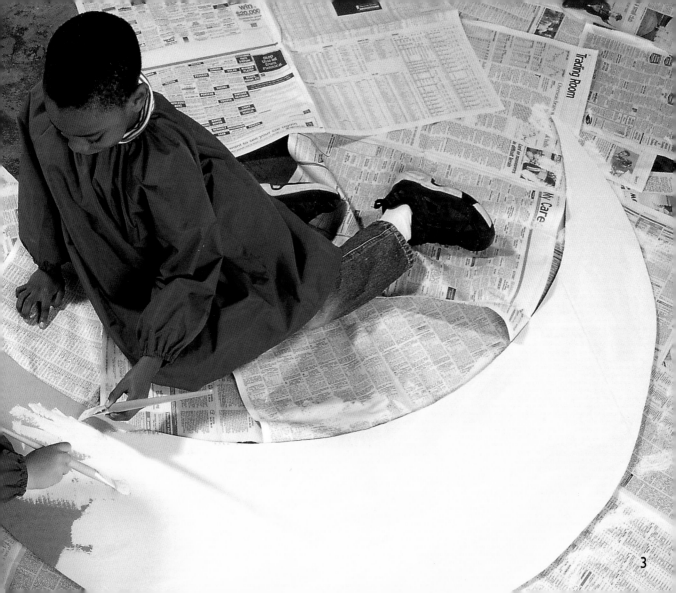

3

Look at us.

We are cutting.

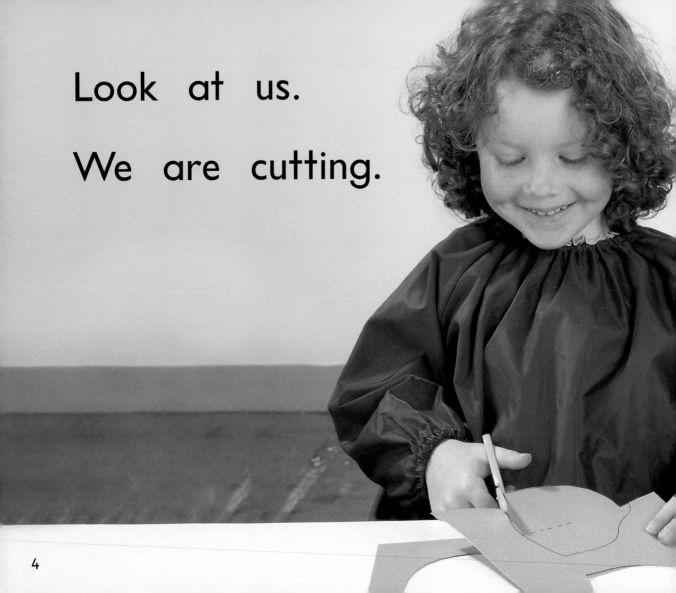

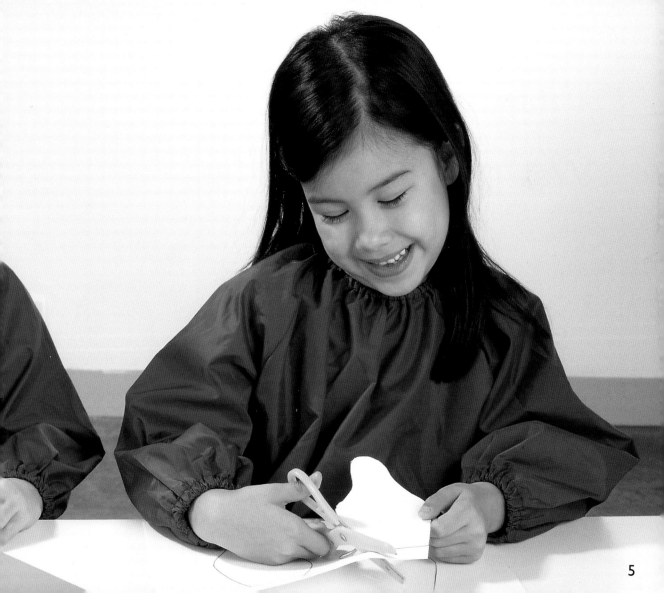

Look at us.

We are dressing up.

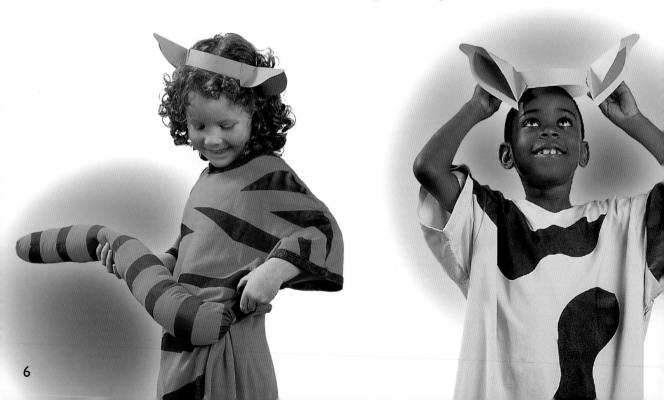

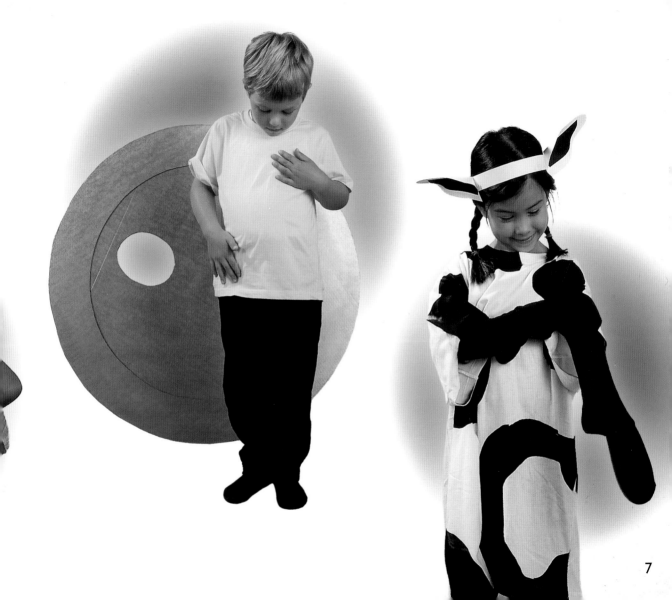

Look at us.

We are dancing.

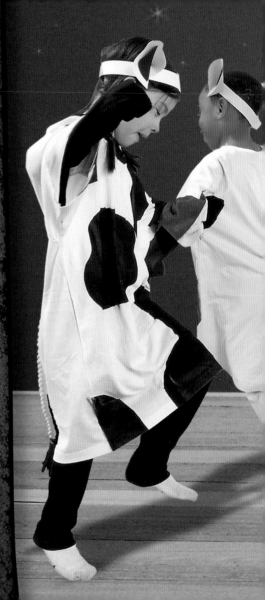

Look at us.

We are singing.

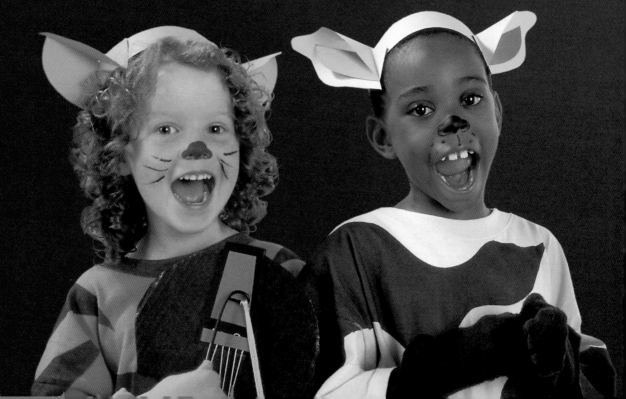

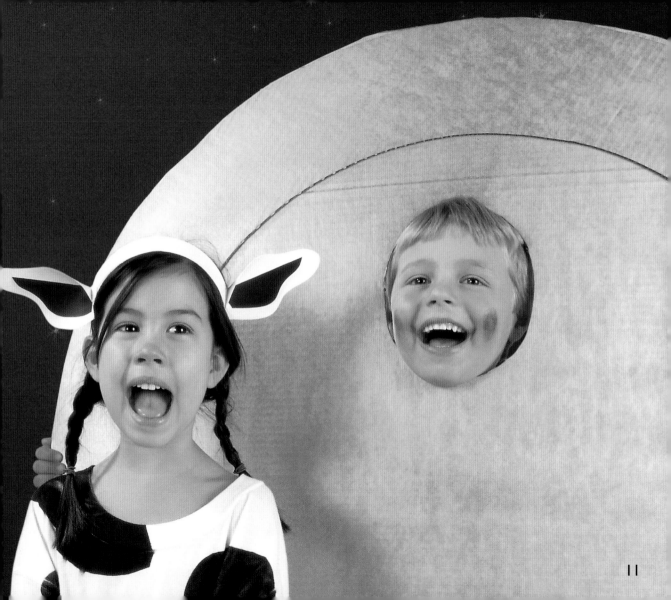

Look at us.

We are clapping.

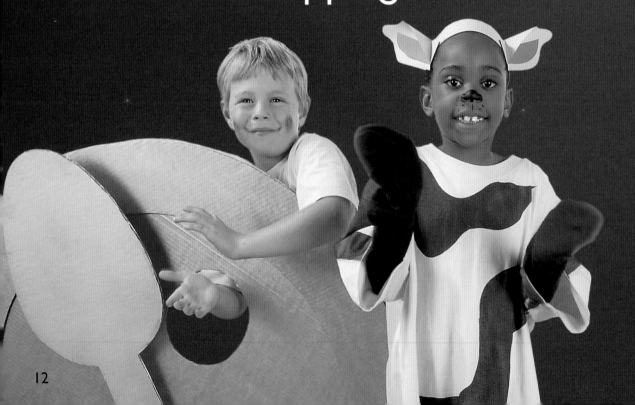

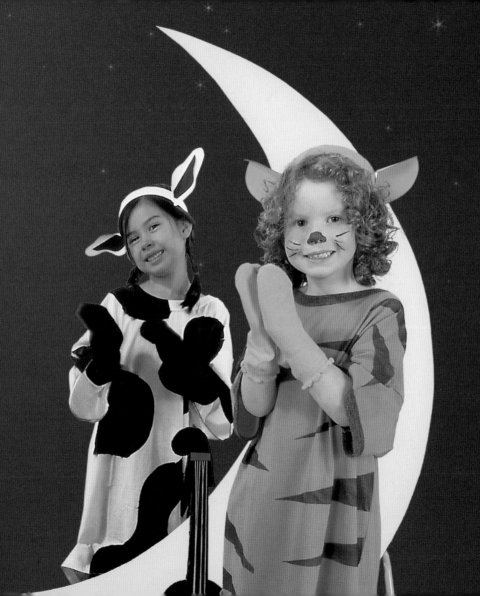

Look at us.

We are smiling.

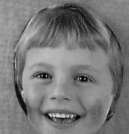

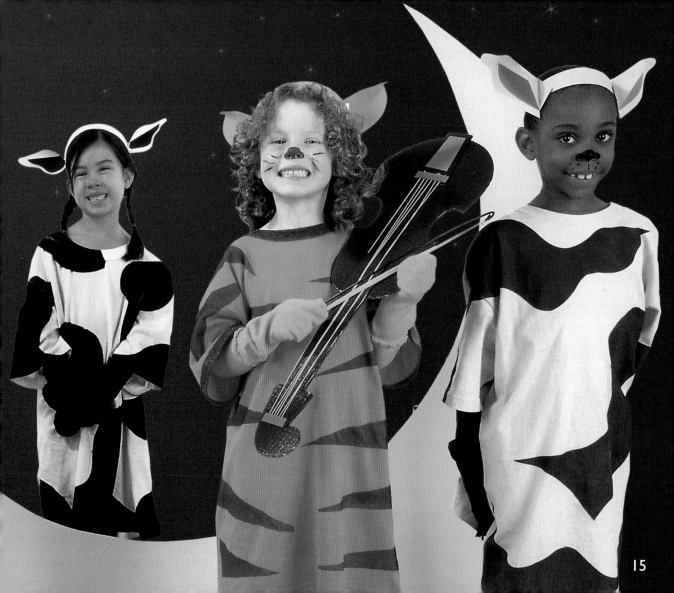

Look at us.

We are waving.

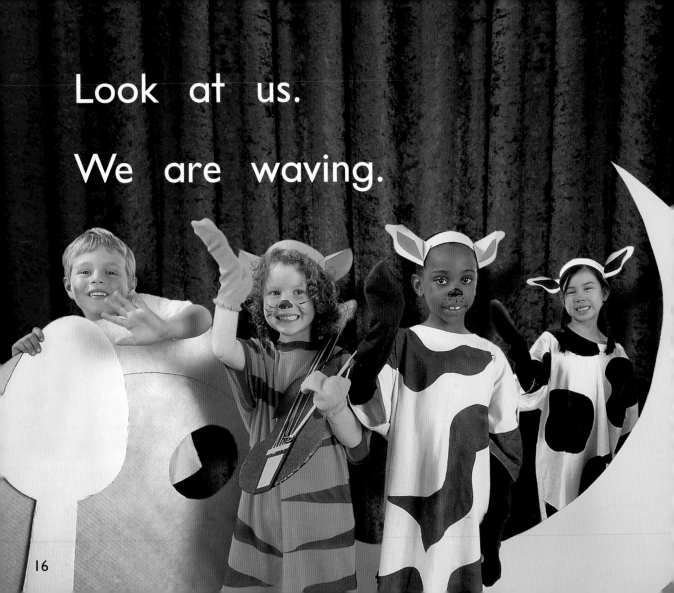